ABOUT THE BANK STREET READY-TO-READ SERIES

Seventy years of educational research and innovative teaching have given the Bank Street College of Education the reputation as America's most trusted name in early childhood education.

Because no two children are exactly alike in their development, we have designed the *Bank Street Ready-to-Read* series in three levels to accommodate the individual stages of reading readiness of children ages four through eight.

- *Level 1:* GETTING READY TO READ—read-alouds for children who are taking their first steps toward reading.
- *Level 2:* READING TOGETHER—for children who are just beginning to read by themselves but may need a little help.
- *Level 3:* I CAN READ IT MYSELF—for children who can read independently.

Our three levels make it easy to select the books most appropriate for a child's development and enable him or her to grow with the series step by step. The *Bank Street Ready-to-Read* books also overlap and reinforce each other, further encouraging the reading process.

We feel that making reading fun and enjoyable is the single most important thing that you can do to help children become good readers. And we hope you'll be a part of Bank Street's long tradition of learning through sharing.

The Bank Street College of Education

For William Robert Davies
—W.H.H.

For Karin
—P.C.

THE GRUFF BROTHERS
A Bantam Little Rooster Book
Simultaneous paper-over-board and trade paper editions/April 1990

Little Rooster is a trademark of Bantam Books,
a division of Bantam Doubleday Dell Publishing Group, Inc.

Series graphic design by Alex Jay/Studio J
Associate Editors: Gwendolyn Smith, Gillian Bucky

Special thanks to James A. Levine, Betsy Gould,
and Erin B. Gathrid.

Library of Congress Cataloging-in-Publication Data
Hooks, William H.
The Gruff brothers / by William H. Hooks ;
illustrated by Pierre Cornuel.
p.   cm. — (Bank Street ready-to-read)
''A Bantam little rooster book.''
''A Byron Preiss book.''
Summary: Three clever billy goats outwit a big,
ugly troll in this classic tale told in rebus format.
ISBN 0-553-05855-X.— ISBN 0-553-34848-5 (pbk.)
[1. Fairy tales.   2. Folklore—Norway.   3. Rebuses.]
I. Cornuel, Pierre, ill.   II. Title.   III. Series.
PZ8.H77Gr   1990
398.24'5297358'09481—dc20
[E]

89-37776   CIP   AC

Bantam Books are published by Bantam Books, a division of Bantam Doubleday
Dell Publishing Group, Inc. Its trademark, consisting of the words ''Bantam Books''
and the portrayal of a rooster, is Registered in U.S. Patent and Trademark Office
and in other countries. Marca Registrada. Bantam Books, 666 Fifth Avenue, New
York, New York 10103.

PRINTED IN THE UNITED STATES OF AMERICA

0 9 8 7 6 5 4 3 2 1

Bank Street Ready-to-Read™

The Gruff Brothers

by William H. Hooks
Illustrated by Pierre Cornuel

A Byron Preiss Book

A BANTAM LITTLE ROOSTER BOOK
NEW YORK · TORONTO · LONDON · SYDNEY · AUCKLAND

There once was a meadow full of animals. There was . . .

a red fox,

a green snake,

a white sheep,

a yellow duck,

a blue bird,

and **3** billy goats.

They were brothers,

and their last name was Gruff

The animals called the **brown** billy goat Little Gruff because he was the smallest.

They called the **black** billy goat Middle Gruff because he was bigger than Little Gruff.

They called the **black** and /white/

billy goat Fiddle Gruff

because he played the fiddle.

He was the biggest of the brothers

and had long pointy horns.

The brothers spent their days

eating sweet green  grass

and tasty yellow flowers.

But at night, big Fiddle Gruff

would play his fiddle,

and all the animals would dance.

The  fox and snake

made a funny couple.

The bird flapped her wings.
The sheep and duck
whirled around
and around.

Little Gruff and

Middle Gruff tap-danced

while Fiddle Gruff played.

Their  feet went *trip-trap!*

Trip-trap! Trip-trap!

But before too long,

all the sweet green  grass

and the tasty yellow flowers

were eaten up.

The animals were soon too hungry
and too tired to dance.

One day Little Gruff said,

"Look at that  bridge.

I see sweet green grass

and tasty yellow flowers

on the other side of the river.

Let's go over the bridge!"

"I wouldn't!"

shouted the red fox.

"Don't!"

said the green snake.

"Wait!"

said the white sheep.

"Hold on!"

said the yellow duck.

"You can't do that!"

said the blue bird.

"Why not?" asked Little Gruff.

"Because," said Middle Gruff.

"Because why?" asked Little Gruff.

"Because a wicked troll guards

the bridge," said Fiddle Gruff.

"What's a troll?" asked Little Gruff.

"I'll tell you," said his big brother.

"He has eyes as big as saucers.

He has a nose as long

and crooked as a snake.

He has teeth

like a tiger's,

and green shaggy hair."

All of the animals were afraid
of the troll.

But Little Gruff said, "I am going
over the  bridge."

Trip-trap! Trip-trap!

He started over.

The troll roared,

Who's that trip-trapping over my bridge?

"It's only me, Little Gruff.

I'm going over the 🌉 bridge

to eat green 🌿 grass."

roared the  troll.
"Oh, no! Don't eat me,"
said Little Gruff.
"I'm much too small.
Wait until Middle Gruff crosses.
He's much bigger than I am."
"Oh, pickles and popcorn,"
said the troll.

"You are much too small.
Go on over the bridge."

So Little Gruff went across—
trip-trap, trip-trap—
and into the meadow.
There he began to eat
sweet green  grass
and tasty yellow flowers.

"I can fool that  troll, too,"
said Middle Gruff.
Trip-trap! Trip-trap!
He started over the ⊔_⊔ bridge.
The troll roared,

Who's that
trip-trapping over
my bridge?

"It's only me, Middle Gruff.
And I am looking
for sweet green  grass."

I am going to
gobble you up!

"Don't do that," said Middle Gruff.
"I'm too small.

Wait until Fiddle Gruff crosses.
He's much bigger than I am."
"Oh, pickles and popcorn!"
roared the troll.

"I am very, very hungry.
And you are too small.
Go on across."

Soon, great big Fiddle Gruff saw
his brothers eating
sweet green  grass
on the other side
of the bridge.

Trip-trap! Trip-trap!
He raced onto the bridge.

The  troll roared,
"Who's that trip-trapping
over my bridge?"
"It's me, Fiddle Gruff,
and I'm very, very hungry."
"Me, too," roared the troll.
"I'm going to gobble you up."

The troll's eyes as big

as saucers were popping.

His nose as long

as a crooked snake

was twitching.

His teeth like a tiger's

were grinding as he roared.

Big Fiddle Gruff was afraid.

He wanted to run.

But he didn't turn back.

Instead, he lowered his

long pointy  horns.

And he butted the  troll
with all his might.

The troll flew off the bridge
and tumbled back into the river.

The last anyone saw of him,
he was swimming away as fast
as his shaggy green arms
could paddle.

Then . . .

the **red**  fox,

the **green** snake,

the **white** sheep,

the **yellow** duck,

and the **blue** bird

all rushed across the bridge.

They ate sweet **green** grass

and tasty **yellow** flowers all day.

That night, when the  stars
came out
and the moon
was bright,
Fiddle Gruff played his fiddle
while . . . the fox,

the  snake, the sheep, the duck, and the bird flapped and clapped.

And Middle Gruff and Little Gruff tap-danced.

Trip-trap! Trip-trap! Trip-trap!

William H. Hooks is the author of many books for children, including the highly acclaimed *Moss Gown*. He is also the Director of Publications at Bank Street College. As part of Bank Street's Media Group, he has been closely involved with such projects as the well-known Bank Street Readers and Discoveries: An Individualized Reading Program. Mr. Hooks lives with three cats in a Greenwich Village brownstone in New York City.

Pierre Cornuel attended the Ecole Superieure d'Arts Modernes and currently resides in Paris, France. He has illustrated more than 20 books for children since 1980 and was a featured illustrator at the Bologna Book Fair in 1987 and 1988. This is Mr. Cornuel's first book for an American audience.